# Lily Tames the Angry Monster

by Daddy Dan

# This book belongs to:

_____

Hello there! My name is Lily! It'll be my bedtime soon.
But for now I'm on mommy's tablet, watching my cartoon.
You and me are just alike! We both like toys and snacks and YouTube shows.
But there's something that I do not like; it's when my mom says «no.»

For example, when I'm watching cartoons all throughout the day,
Then my mommy makes me stop and says, «Your eyes should take a break!»
I don't like to hear those words. They make me shout and scream and cry.
And before I even know it, I feel angry deep inside!

PARENTS: «Do you know what anger is?»

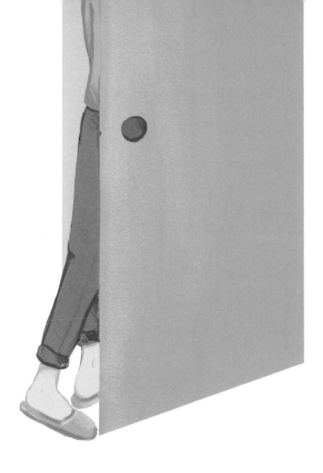

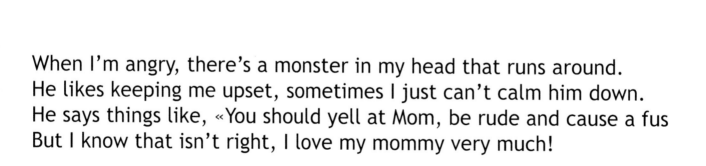

When I'm angry, there's a monster in my head that runs around.
He likes keeping me upset, sometimes I just can't calm him down.
He says things like, «You should yell at Mom, be rude and cause a fus
But I know that isn't right, I love my mommy very much!

Even still, I hear his words. They dance around inside my head.
I don't like this angry monster; he is mean and loud and red.
But the angrier I get, the more my monster grows inside.
He is glad when things annoy me; he won't let my anger hide!

PARENTS: «What things annoy you? Draw them near Lily's angry things!»

I got angry once again when it was time to take a bath.
Mommy tried to wash my hair but I said, «No! I don't like that!»
For the water was too cold, and some shampoo got in my eye.
Even though this pleased my monster, I was mad enough to cry!

Later on inside the kitchen, I got really, really mad.
Mommy tried to feed me broccoli...she KNOWS I don't like that!
So I threw it on the ground! My mom was shocked at what I'd done.
But my monster started laughing, for he thought that he had won!

PARENTS: «Do you see a monster when you get angry?
If not, what do you see?»

When I crossed my arms in anger, and had turned myself away,
That's when mommy came to hug me, and she had nice words to say.
I could see this scared the monster, for he knows my mom is wise.
She is smart enough to help me take this monster down in size!

«Lily, honey, are you seeing a red monster run about?»
«Why, yes, Mommy! But I wonder, how'd you ever find that out?»
«Well, my dear, there's something similar between both me and you.
I could tell you saw a monster, because I have got one too!»

CHILDREN: Ask your parents, «What makes you angry? Do you get angry a lot? How does your monster make you feel?»

I was shocked to hear her say this, for my mommy is so kind!
She says anyone can get upset, it happens all the time.
«Well, if everyone gets angry, can it really be that mean?»
«Let me show you, little Lily! Take a look at this daydream.»

I looked up inside her «thought cloud» and I saw a crying boy.
He was sad because I'd yelled at him and pulled away his toy.
«Even though you think your angry monster lives inside your head,
He can do bad things to others, which makes pain and sadness spread.»

PARENTS: «When is the last time you were angry? Did your monster do something mean to someone else?»

CHILDREN: Ask your parents, «Has your monster ever done anything mean to someone else?»

«You are right about that, Mommy! This can happen, now I see!
If I don't control my monster, look how rude he'll try to be!»
«It's okay to have your feelings, Lily. They are from inside.
But make sure you always share them; do not let them try to hide!»

It was time for me to learn how I cannot get mad at others.
It felt like I was at school, except the teacher was my mother!
She got out a giant blackboard that was rolled about by wheels.
It was filled with tips to help me understand the things I feel.

PARENTS: «When your monster is nearby, what do you see, hear, and feel?»

When my mommy's monster starts to wake, she doesn't break a sweat.
For she knows he'll try to look for things to make her get upset.
So when accidents around her make the monster start to rise,
Mommy calms him down by starting up her breathing exercise.

With her eyes shut tight, she takes a breath, and then she lets it out.
When she's finished, she starts over, and that helps her not to shout.
Breathing in and breathing out will make her monster rest a while.
After that, she can replace her anger with a happy smile!

PARENTS: "Try this breathing exercise with me! Breathe in on 1, breathe out on 2. Breathe in on 3, breathe out on 4. Breathe in on 5, breathe out on 6. Breathe in on 7, breathe out on 8. Breathe in on 9, breathe out on 10. Do you feel calm now?"

CHILDREN: Ask your parents, «What else can I do to feel calm?»

Now I know what I should do when I feel angry with a person.
I should breathe and count to ten so that the problem doesn't worsen!
That will make my monster sleep, and it will also work for you!
Wouldn't it be great if EVERYONE could tame their monster, too?

«You are right! If that could happen, it would really change the world. But you know, there are many monsters inside every boy and girl!»
«That's amazing! Will these other monsters cause a big commotion?»
«Not at all! They're 'happy,' 'curious,' or 'sad.' They're called EMOTIONS.»

PARENTS: What other emotions do you know about?

CHILDREN: Ask your parents: "Are there anymore emotions out there?"

Hello there! My name is Lily! It'll be my bedtime soon.
I have cleaned up all my toys, and I've sat down to watch cartoons.
When my mommy comes and tells me that my eyes should have a rest,
I look inside my sleeping monster and say, «Yes, Mommy, yes!»

Thanks to Mommy, I have tamed the angry monster in my head.
But the other monsters scare me, and they fill my mind with dread!
Mommy says that this is FEAR, but that it shouldn't make me worry.
She will teach me how to handle it and stop it in a hurry!

My next lesson is to deal with fear! You want to take a look?
That's fantastic! We will learn about it in the next book!

Made in the USA
Columbia, SC
11 August 2020